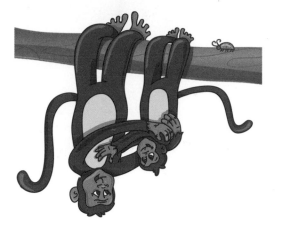

My Mother Is My Friend

by Kimberly P. Johnson

Illustrated by Zoe Ranucci

Best of luck
in life!
You are great!

Kimberly P.
Jo...

Visit the author at: www.simplycreativeworks.com

This book is dedicated to the people in my life who were always a "Mother" to me.
Knowing that there are too many to mention - I love you all!!

To my "Mama" Lucy - who was the anchor in my life and more than a grandmother - her memory
will live in my heart forever. She is the reason I am!!

To Sue and Helen - thank you for teaching me to be a caring person
you both gave me something special in my life.

To Ezra Bridges - I love you beyond words.
You are the angel that I don't see everyday, but I know that you are there.

To Jeff - my mentor and my friend. You help keep me grounded. I love you always!!!

Zoe - What can I say? You amaze me every time. You are a talented artist and a joy to work with.
Thank you, again!!
KPJ

Thank you Kim for another fun and challenging project! To my mom, I am so grateful for the wonderful
relationship and friendship we have always had. To Ginny, you are not only one of the greatest friends I will have in
this lifetime... you are also like a second mom to me. And to my Mila, there is nothing I love more than being your
mother and I so look forward to the days where we are the best of friends.
ZR

First Edition

Edited by Simply Creative Works

Designed and Typeset by Zoe Ranucci, www.gooddharma.com

Printed by RR Donnelley
McAllen, TX

Printed in Mexico
ISBN 0-9713334-6-7

"My Mother Is My Friend" is a warm-hearted book that reminds us of the joy and appreciation that flows from Mother to child. With caring as the foundation, each mother in this book experiences pride while watching her little ones grow-up. The underlying messages also depict the commitment and dedication of mothers. "My Mother Is My Friend" reminds us to appreciate the gifts that we are given from unselfish and loving family members. Written in a wonderful, rhythmic style, this book captures the attention and hearts of all who read it. It is a book that everyone will love for years to come! Kimberly P. Johnson draws from her own experiences of having a loving and wonderful "Mother" who not only protected her throughout life but taught her valuable lessons that she carries with her daily. Kimberly states: "I want children and parents to realize the importance of connecting and creating a more sharing spirit. It is this generous and trusting love that creates a friendship - one that lasts a lifetime."

My mother is my friend –
we swim the ocean and the sea.

My mother is my friend –
she always kisses me.

My mother is my friend –
I bet she could lift a ton.

My mother is my friend —
she makes my bath time really fun.

My mother is my friend –
she's the fastest one around.

My mother is my friend –
her feet hardly touch the ground.

6

My mother is my friend –
her wings spread across the sky.

My mother is my friend —
she inspires me to try.

8

My mother is my friend —
she can reach the tallest tree.

9

My mother is my friend –
she gives tasty leaves to me.

My mother is my friend —
she has fur that is silky black.

11

My mother is my friend –
she lets me ride on her back.

My mother is my friend –
she roars very loud.

13

My mother is my friend –
I'll try to make her proud.

My mother is my friend –
she likes to swing on trees.

My mother is my friend –
we hang from our knees.

My mother is my friend –
she watches everything I do.

My mother is my friend –
I'm her favorite little roo.

18

My mother is my friend –
she's the smartest one I know.

My mother is my friend –
she knows exactly where to go.

My mother is my friend –
I like to watch her reach.

21

My mother is my friend –
she takes the time to teach.

22

My mother is my friend –
there is nothing she can't hear.

23

My mother is my friend –
I'm her special little deer.

24

My mother is my friend –
she's never too tired to play.

My mother is my friend –
she loves me everyday!!

My mother is my friend –
she's a strong and wooly llama.

27

My mother is my friend –
but I just call her Mama!

28

The End